MW01016246

# Annie Bizzanni

Story: France Hallé
Illustrations: Fil et Julie

Owl
kids

Translation: Sarah Cummins

**Annie Bizzanni** likes to try everything! She starts lots of projects but she never finishes any of them.

**Annie Bizzanni** lives in a very large house. One day she decides to get out her tools and make it even bigger.

She moves her kitchen **cupboards**, knocks down a **wall** or two, puts a new **doorway** here, an extra **window** there, and gets to work **painting** and **wallpapering**. Annie starts lots of home renovations. But she doesn't finish any of them.

That means the **kitchen** doesn't have any cupboards,
the **walls** still have holes in them, and her
**bedroom** is only half wallpapered. What a mess!

Her friends laugh at her half-finished house projects,
but they like **Annie Bizzanni** just the way she is.

**Annie Bizzanni** loves to sew. *She likes to try everything!* Every year she makes Halloween costumes for all her friends. In September, she picks out **fabric**, thread, **buttons**, and pompoms.

She makes four costumes at once – it's so much faster that way! She **measures** and **snips**. She **stitches** and **rips**.... But every year, on Halloween, the costumes are not finished.

The **leopard** has no tail!

The beautiful **princess** has no skirt!

The **vampire** has no black cape!

The **rabbit** has no ears!

Her friends laugh at her silly costumes, but they like **Annie Bizzanni** just the way she is.

**Annie Bizzanni** loves to read. *She likes to try everything!*

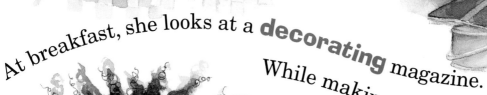

At breakfast, she looks at a **decorating** magazine.

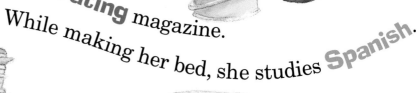

While making her bed, she studies **Spanish**.

At lunchtime, she races through a guide to **astronomy**.

While waiting at a stoplight, she reads the **newspaper**.

In the garden, she leafs through
a **car repair** manual.

At dinner, she devours
a book on **science**.

In her bath, she dives
into a **mystery**.

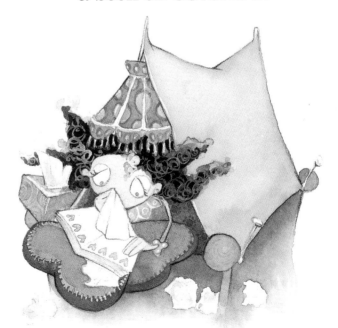

At bedtime, she snuggles
up with a **novel**.

**Annie Bizzanni** starts to read lots of things. But she never finishes any of them. So, Annie still doesn't understand Spanish. She has no idea how any of her books end. And she doesn't know that on page 23 of the newspaper it says she's a dangerous driver.

Her friends laugh at all the books she never finishes, but they like **Annie Bizzanni** just the way she is.

**Annie Bizzanni** always invites her friends over for dinner. She adores cooking. *She likes to try everything!* She chooses a **menu**, she sets the **table**, she cuts up the **vegetables**, and she starts **cooking**, but…

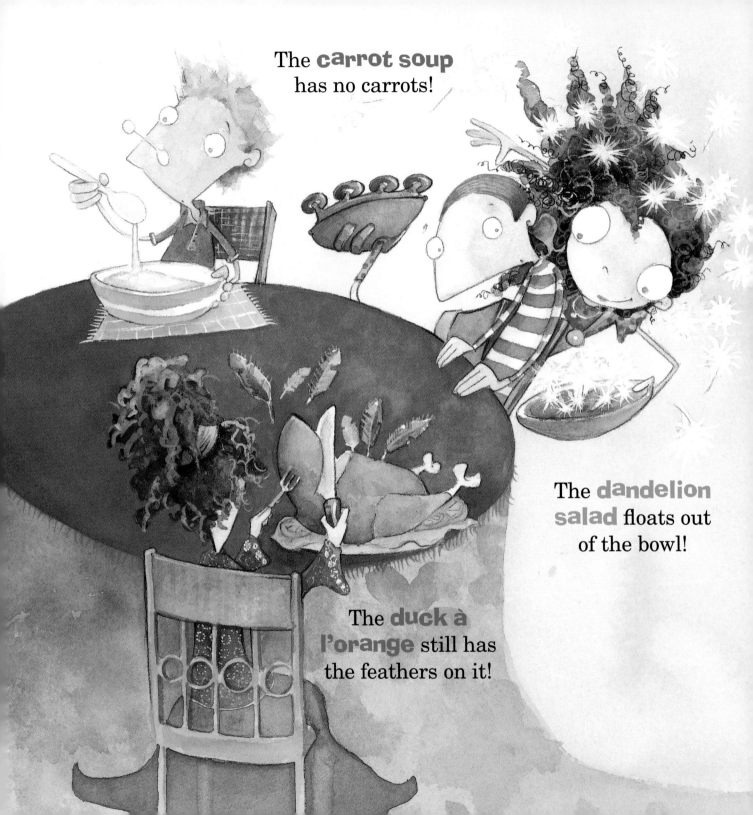

The **carrot soup** has no carrots!

The **dandelion salad** floats out of the bowl!

The **duck à l'orange** still has the feathers on it!

And when she makes **flambéed bananas**, the house nearly catches on fire – and the bananas are burnt to a crisp!

Her friends laugh at the spoiled dinners, but they like **Annie Bizzanni** just the way she is.

**Annie Bizzanni** loves to write stories. *She likes to try everything!*

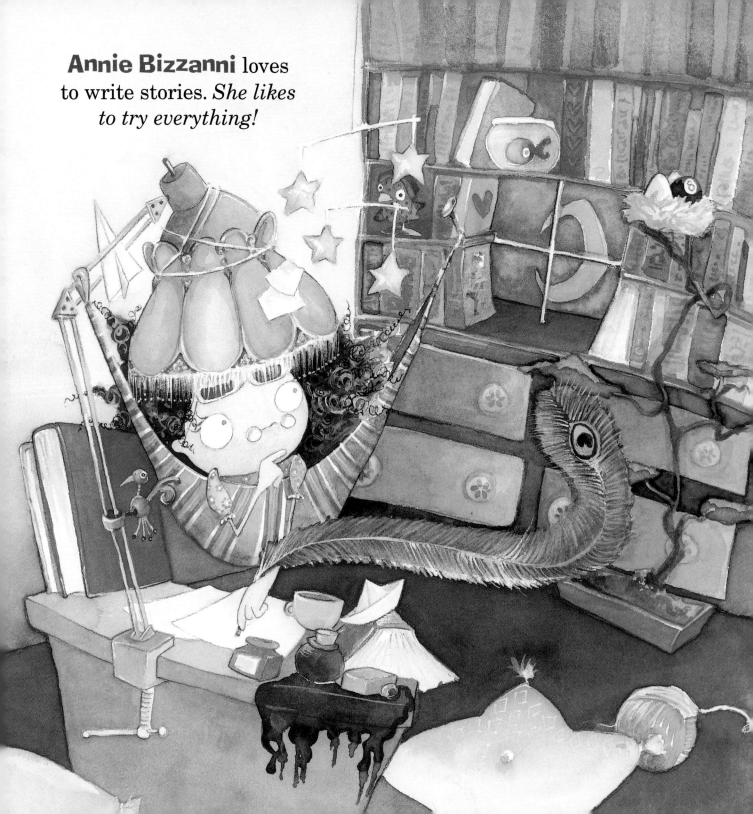

Here is her latest **story**:

Once upon a time, in a
garden filled with flowers,
there lived two butterflies who
spent their time flitting about
on the sweetly-scented breeze.
One day, the two butterflies
met a little lost ladybug.

But what did the **butterflies** do next?

**Annie Bizzanni** doesn't know.
Before she finished her story, she
went on a **trip**. She loves to travel.
*She likes to try everything!*

Her friends laugh
at the silly things she does, but
they like **Annie Bizzanni**
just the way she is.